LiLac peabody

and
Charlie Chase

Also by Annie Dalton:

Lilac Peabody and Sam Sparks
Lilac Peabody and Bella Bright

The *Angels Unlimited* series:

Lilac Peabody

and
Charlie Chase

ANNIE DALTON

illustrated by Griff

HarperCollins *Children's Books*

To Sophie and Izzie with love

First published in Great Britain by HarperCollins *Children's Books* in 2005
HarperCollins *Children's Books* is a division of HarperCollins*Publishers* Ltd
77-85 Fulham Palace Road, Hammersmith, London W6 8JB

The HarperCollins *Children's Books* website address is
www.harpercollinschildrensbooks.co.uk

1 3 5 7 9 8 6 4 2

Text copyright © Annie Dalton 2005
Illustrations © Andrew Griffin 2005

ISBN 0 00 713773 7

Printed and bound in England by
Clays Ltd, St Ives plc

1.
GRRRKKK!

This story starts with my brain.

Ninety-nine per cent of the time it works fine: like when I'm playing football. I'm *brilliant* at football. My mates say I'm the best defender our school ever had. But I'm not just some sports nut (though I *am* pretty nutty!). I'm also an ace problem solver. No, seriously! If there's a glitch in your computer, just call in Charlie Chase! My teacher says I'm like a bloodhound, because I don't give up until I've got the answer.

So you see, most of the time my brain lives a happy, useful life.

Just don't ask it to read!

"GRRRKKK!"

Ever heard someone try to start an old car on a cold winter's day?

Exactly the same thing happens to my brain when it sees print! It doesn't even have to be a whole page. It can be one line like: "Honey Hope's pants are on fire!"

If my mate Sam saw that sentence, his brain would instantly send him a mad cartoon of our school bully with flames spurting from her bum!

But my brain's a bit wonky, so I never get the cartoon; I just see lots of letters hopping about like pesky little fleas. I could stare at them till I had a long grey beard and my brain would STILL be going "GRRRKKK!"

OK, having reading problems is a pain, but, like Sam says, "You're just dyslexic, Charlie. It's not like you've got three heads!" Of course some kids think "dyslexic" is just another word for "no brain". I tell them: "Hey, don't knock the brain. This brain is pure quality!"

It's true. How many people remember their first words? I remember mine *exactly*. Most babies start off with little words like mumma, dadda, teddy. My first words were "fire engine"!

My parents were convinced they'd produced a boy genius, but I was just mad about fire engines! I was mad about loads of things when I was little: earth worms, power sockets…

I was a right little daredevil. When I was four years old I climbed up a stepladder in my Superman cape and tried to fly!

My parents rushed to pick me up but I didn't have a scratch on me. I told them Lilac Peabody saved me with her Special Powers.

Lilac Peabody was my invisible friend (well, invisible to everyone but me). I've got a splodgy painting I did of her at playgroup. I'm not sure if she was an actual space alien, or if I just ran out of paint, because I painted her skin the strangest mix of blue and green!

I forgot all about my little magic buddy once I started school and had some real buddies to play with. By the time this story starts, I'm a healthy, non-flying, non-worm-eating ten year old.

My fave food is Spaghetti Bolognese, my fave colour is blue, and I love any music I can dance to. I'm a *wicked* dancer! And, even if I say so myself, I'm the most popular kid in my school. Everybody wants to be mates with Charlie Chase.

I should be happy, right?

I *am* happy when I'm at school. Everyone adores me at school. I make everyone laugh, including my teacher. I even make Honey Hope laugh and she's the most evil girl in the galaxy. School is not a problem.

My problems start when it's time to go home.

Other kids race out of school as if they can't wait to see their families. I just trudge along like a zombie. And when I get home, I don't go straight in. I hang around outside for ages, kicking bits of brick out of our garden wall.

I tell myself off sometimes. "Why are you lurking outside like a little lost puppy?" I ask myself. "Your family are not monsters. They care about you."

This is true. It just doesn't help.

Finally I take a deep breath, turn my key in the lock and go in. The house is spookily silent.

I peep round the sitting room door. Everyone's home: my mum, my dad, my big sister, Jessie, and my baby sister, Martha.

They're in the exact same positions as yesterday *and* the day before that…

Jessie is lying on the rug by the fire. My parents are at opposite ends of the sofa. Baby Martha is sitting at their feet. No one speaks. No one even moves – except to turn a page.

My friends' families do loads of different things when they get home: kick a ball around the garden, make popcorn, play with the puppy.

My family just reads.

Then a strange thing happens. Dad looks up and sees me in the doorway and BING! Everyone springs to life.

Dad puts on his jolliest voice. "Charlie, you're back!"

"How was school?" Mum asks me in *her* jolliest voice.

"OK," I mumble.

"Just OK?" says Mum. "So what did you do today?"

I shift my feet. "Nothing much."

"You must have done *something*."

"Not really."

Mum gives me an extra-friendly smile. "So, erm – did you finish your reading book?"

I shrug as if I don't care. "No."

"You'll get there, Charlie," says Dad in his super-jolly voice.

"I can't believe he's *still* reading that book," Jessie sounds smug.

"Well, I am," I say, "so get over it."

"Ooh, *touchy*!" she says.

"Now, now," Dad tells her. "Your brother's good at other things."

"My brother's a moody pig," Jessie says under her breath.

"I am *not* moody," I snarl.

The baby gives a worried whimper.

"He's such a liar," Jessie tells my parents. "We're just sitting reading peacefully, then he comes home and picks a fight."

"I am NOT picking a FIGHT!" I yell.

Little Martha's mouth goes completely square, then she just howls.

"Oh, Charlie," says Mum, shaking her head. "You scared the baby."

"You should watch that temper, Charlie," says Dad. "It'll get you into trouble."

"Will everyone just leave me ALONE!" I yell.

I rush upstairs to my room and push open the window. I hang my head out, taking gulps of air.

Can you see why I hate coming home?

To my family, I'm not problem-solving Charlie, or Charlie the football hero. I'm not even Charlie the comedian.

I'm just the Boy Who Can't Read.

But it's not just my family who make me feel trapped. Did I explain about the books? What's the WORST place a dyslexic kid could possibly live?

A bookshop, right?

2.
THE PUZZLE TREE

My parents run a mail-order business; they sell second-hand books. Unfortunately they can't afford a proper shop, so they have to store all the books in our house. We've got books on

the landing. We've even got books in our toilet!

I HATE going to the loo in the night. I know it's stupid, but I feel like the books are sneering at me. I can almost hear their little voices going: *Nur-nur nee-nur-nur. Charlie can't read us. He doesn't belong in this family.*

It's true. I'm like the wonky peg in Martha's hammer pegs.

No matter how hard everyone tries to squish me into shape, I don't fit.

Mum and Dad really worry about me. That's why they decided to send me to see a counsellor. I'm supposed to go to his office every Monday after school and tell him any problems that might be interfering with my reading – apart from my wonky brain, I mean!

I don't really mind going to see a counsellor. It's not like it's hard work. Plus, my parents are paying Dr Fell a lot of money, so I do my best to keep him happy. He likes to hear about my dreams for some reason, so every week I make up an action-packed nightmare. I put in heaps of scary details to make it convincing, and he always seems gripped.

If I was Dr Fell, I'd move my office to a decent building. You should see the state of his walls: cracks and damp patches everywhere. If I

squint, some of the cracks look like one of those magic trees in puzzle books, with friendly monsters hiding in the branches. Every week I squint until I find a new monster.

I'm not meant to be monster-spotting, obviously. I'm meant to be telling my darkest secrets to Dr Fell, so he can fix my problems and turn me into a happy little bookworm like the rest of my family.

Unfortunately I don't have any dark secrets.

One afternoon I arrive in a thunderstorm to find my counsellor's ceiling has sprung a leak. Most people would call in a builder. Dr Fell has just stuck his bin underneath to catch the drips.

I drape my coat on the radiator to dry, then I stretch myself out on the couch. First I tell Dr Fell about my week, then I describe my latest rambly "dream".

He sounds worried. "So Charlie, how did it make you *feel* when the book bomb destroyed all the books in your house?"

"The book bomb wasn't *my* invention," I remind him super-fast. "It was the mad scientist's. Didn't I mention that?"

No answer. When I sneak a look, Dr Fell has got his eyes closed. He looks depressed. He's getting fed up with me, I think.

I try to take my mind off things with a game of Spot the Monster. I squint until I'm cross-eyed, but I can't improve on my grand total of six. Six monsters. That means I've been coming for six sessions. Six sessions and I still can't read. No wonder everyone thinks I'm a hopeless case.

How did my life turn into this mess? Why couldn't I just stay four years old for ever? Then I could still believe in Lilac Peabody.

No matter what went wrong, Lilac could fix it. If my parents forgot to plug in my night-light, she'd just put magic glowing stars on my ceiling. If I fell down and hurt my knee, she'd do some nutty stunt to cheer me up, like filling the entire house with teeny-tiny humming birds.

Stop it! I tell myself. Ten year olds don't need night-lights and they definitely don't need imaginary friends to solve their problems.

Suddenly I don't care. Crazy longing whooshes through me and the words pop out all by themselves: "*I wish Lilac Peabody was here!*"

I don't shout my wish out loud, I just whisper it to the monsters in the puzzle tree. But it has the most amazing effect. *FITZZ!* There's a fizzing sound like someone lighting a sparkler, and the tree begins to change.

The branches sprout real leaves. I can hear them whispering in the breeze. And the monsters are growing scales and claws. Six pairs of glowing eyes watch me through the leaves.

That's not all.

A new creature is looking down at me from the puzzle tree. She's not exactly a monster, but she's not exactly human either. She's too small and shimmery and her eyes are much too wise.

"I don't know what you're doing here, Charlie," she says firmly, "but you're going to leave this *minute*."

It's Lilac Peabody.

3.
THUNDER AND LIGHTNING

I gabble something to Dr Fell, I don't know what, everything happens so fast. Lilac Peabody flits down from the ceiling then we charge out of his office.

Lilac heads straight for the staircase. "There's an empty office upstairs!"

We zoom up to the next level. This office is in a worse state than Dr Fell's. Rain is pouring through the skylight. An assortment of pans and buckets stand underneath to catch the water.

With the thunder, the rain hammering on the glass, and the bingy-bongy buckets, the noise is deafening.

We both start talking at once.

"Did you really hear my wish?" I ask her.

"Didn't you love the tree!" Lilac giggles.

We both go, "Oh, sorry!"

Then we do this nutty handshake we used to do. We're so happy to see each other, we can't stop smiling.

"The tree was super-cool," I agree. "Especially the monsters."

Lilac sucks in her cheeks and imitates their mad stares.

"Dr Fell didn't see them?" I say anxiously. "Yikes, I hope he didn't see *you*!"

She laughs. "Grown-ups don't notice anything. Remember those humming birds?"

She's just the same; she still wears glittery clothes that look like they've been nicked off a fairy's washing line, and she still plaits strange things into her hair. It's seashells today. I try to imagine where you'd find shells that small.

Lilac is looking worried. "Charlie, why *are* your parents sending you to Dr Fell? Don't get me wrong, he's an excellent counsellor. But for kids with problems – not you!"

I feel myself going red. "No. I've got some serious problems. I've really changed since you knew me."

"Dr Fell doesn't think so," Lilac says to my surprise. "He has NO idea why your parents send you to see him. He thinks you're totally fine."

I'm amazed. "You actually read his mind?"

"No, bird-brain, I read his notes," she grins.

"I'm not totally fine," I tell her. "I'm ten years old and I still can't read."

Lilac laughs. "So? Albert Einstein was a total doofus at school. He grew up to be the most famous scientist who ever lived. Anyway, reading is just one problem. You said you'd got loads."

"I don't even know what's wrong with me," I say huskily. "I think I'm probably just weird."

There's a low rumble of thunder like a drum roll. Lilac moves so close, I can see my reflection in her eyes. "I'm your magic buddy, Charlie. You can tell me *anything*."

"This is going to sound stupid," I say at last, "but I hate going home."

Lilac nods as if this makes perfect sense. "Because of the books?"

"Yes, and I get into fights with Jessie. Plus my parents think I hate them because I'm always off with my mates. But…" I suddenly have to swallow. "…then I *do* go home," I gulp, "and they just go on and *on* about my reading. It's like I'm their big project and I've gone wrong. Sometimes I think they'd like to rub me out and start again."

Lilac is completely still. "You think they're ashamed of you?"

I burst into tears.

I did have a dark secret after all and I didn't even know.

Lilac doesn't tell me everything will be OK. She doesn't say a word. For a long while the only sound is me sniffling, and the rain drumming and bonging. Suddenly she flits across the room and points to a nameplate on the door. "Can you read those words?"

I wipe my eyes. "Pr...iv...ate Det..." I spell out slowly. "Does it say Private Detective?" I sniffle hopefully.

She nods. "Do you know why I asked you to read that?"

I give a deep sigh. "To see how bad my reading is?"

"No, you big noodle!" she grins. "Because it's a CLUE! Your first, most important, clue."

I have no idea what she's talking about. "A clue to what?"

"A clue to help us solve the family mystery!" she beams.

FLASH. A zigzag of lightning rips across the sky.

"There *is* a serious problem in your house," Lilac goes on earnestly. "But it has NOTHING to do with you. Just the opposite in fact."

I have no idea what she's on about. It's like she's talking in riddles.

"All I can say is, thank *goodness* your mum and dad have got you to sort them out! Oh, don't worry — I'll help," she adds with a warm smile. "When things get this bad you need at least two."

My head is spinning. "Two…?"

She raps on the nameplate with her shimmery little knuckles. "Two detectives, of course! Didn't I tell you this was your clue?

PRIVATE DETECTIVE

Your family is in trouble, Charlie. We need to work out why, and whenever there's a big mystery, you call in the detectives. Oh, that's us in case you were wondering!" Lilac beams at me. "I think Peabody and Chase will make a pretty good team!"

I'm starting to feel annoyed. "Lilac, I keep telling you, I've changed! I'm not a little kid any more. I haven't just bumped my knee. I need serious help."

Lilac Peabody looks surprised. "I know that."

I take a deep breath. "If you want to help me, you'll have to use your Powers for real."

"I always do," she smiles.

I gasp. "Honestly? You'll really do it? Oh, Lilac, you have no idea… I'll never ask you to do anything again.

But of course I won't need to. All my troubles will be over."

Now Lilac just looks puzzled. "How come? I haven't told you my plan yet."

"Who needs a plan! I just need you to zap my brain so I can read," I say cheerfully. "It'll take you five seconds tops!"

She shakes her head. "I don't zap people. Never have. Never will. Now about the detective thing—"

I'm so disappointed that I totally lose it. "Do you know what you are?" I yell at her. "You're a big FAKER! You say you're my magic buddy, but that's RUBBISH. Did I ask for a million pounds and a mansion? No, I didn't! I just asked for ONE little favour, and you won't even do that. I don't know why you even bothered coming back!"

Lilac sounds completely calm. "I came back to help you fix your family's problems of course. But we have to do it the right way!"

"Will you just stop it!" I shout. "Why do you keep saying *they* need help?"

She smiles. "Because it's the truth. There's certainly nothing wrong with *you!*"

"Are you DEAF? There's *everything* wrong with me. This isn't some little kiddies' *game*, and I don't want to play at being detectives! If you're not going to take me seriously, just go away. I really mean it, Lilac!" I scream at her. "JUST GO AWAY!"

4.
BOOK CRAZY!

I run home through the storm and let myself in.
My temper has died down by this time. Actually,
I feel slightly ashamed of myself.

I can hear stirring and chopping sounds from

the kitchen. Mum and Dad always cook together, but this is my parents, so they're reading at the same time.

I hear Lilac saying, *I came back to help you fix your family's problems.*

She's got it all upside down, I think. They don't have problems. They're the grown-ups. I'm the one who needs the help.

"Hi," I say in my friendliest voice. "Dr Fell didn't phone?"

BING! Mum and Dad spring to attention.

"No, why?" says Mum anxiously.

"What's wrong?" asks Dad.

"Nothing, it's going great!" I fib. "I just thought…" But their noses are already back in their books.

My parents complain that I don't tell them stuff. But if it's not about books, they're not interested.

Like when I was the ring master in our circus project. I was a *brilliant* ring master. Even Bella said I was brilliant and she's an actual circus kid. But my parents didn't want to hear about it. They just ranted about how teachers should stick to teaching the kids to read, because reading is the Key to Everything.

I notice a little voice murmuring under the table. Martha is raiding Mum's handbag. I crouch down for a better look. "What have you got there, Marth? I hope it's not Mum's credit card?"

Martha examines the plastic card carefully. "Lie-ree cart," she corrects.

My jaw drops. "Did you just say library card?"

"Lie-ree cart," she repeats proudly.

I jump up. "Mum? Dad? Did you hear what she just said?"

Mum turns her page, stirring the sauce with her free hand. At the same moment, Dad licks his finger and turns *his* page.

"Hello? Newsflash!" I say loudly. "Your baby just said her first words!"

"Absolutely," Dad murmurs.

Mum blinks like an owl. "What did you say, Charlie?"

I turn cold inside. Everyone's family has their funny little ways, but this is not funny. It's worryingly weird.

I go into the sitting room. Jessie is lying on her tummy, with her nose two inches from her book. "Martha can talk," I announce. "She said 'library card'. Can you believe that?"

Jessie puts her hands over her ears. "Go away, I'm reading."

I go up to my room and sit on the bed.

This can't be happening, I think. It's like they aren't even on the same planet. I can't believe I didn't see it until now.

They're totally book-crazy! If they were TV-crazy, I could just pull out the plug. Of course my parents refuse to own a TV. They say too much TV rots your brains. No one says what too much reading does to you, but I think I know. My family have spent so much time reading, they've forgotten there's a real world. To them, books *are* the world.

I must have the only parents in the solar system who *encourage* their kids to read at the table.

Maybe burnt spaghetti sauce tastes better if you're reading? I think.

Martha has one mouthful then sensibly drops her spoon.

She spots a cat walking along the garden wall. "Meow!" she tells us excitedly.

"Yes, sweetie," murmurs my mum.

Martha tries again. "Meow, meow!"

"Ssh, darling." Dad's voice seems to come from a distant room.

Martha's face crumples. "Meow," she whispers sadly.

I try to remember if meal times in our house ever used to be fun. But I can't, so I try to think of the last time my family all went out together, or had a real talk, but I can't remember that either.

Jessie slams down her book. "Mum, why is Charlie being weird? He's been staring at us all through tea!"

"I was just thinking," I explain.

"Here's my impression of my brother thinking." Jessie scratches her head like an ape. "Duh, this is my left hand," she says in a dopey voice. "So, ah, duh, I *think* this must be my right hand!"

It's like she *wants* to make me mad. I take a deep breath. "I was wondering what you guys would do if we didn't have any books."

"What IS he babbling about?" Jessie asks the air. "Hello? Our parents run a bookshop. We're not likely to run out!"

I want to empty the water jug over her head, but I just say, "Come on, Martha. Let's find that little kitty."

At bedtime Mum comes in to give me a hug. Mum's hugs are a bit lopsided because she needs her middle finger to keep her place in her book.

"I know it's hard for you, Charlie," she says softly. "But it's worth keeping at it, believe me. Reading is just the Key to Everything."

I've heard this speech a million times. But tonight a surprising thought pops into my head. If I didn't have reading problems, what *would* they all talk about?

Lilac's right. This family is in big trouble.

5.
THE DREAM DETECTIVES

I lie awake listening to the swish of the traffic.
Eventually Mum and Dad come upstairs. For a
while I hear pages rustling then the house goes
quiet.

Minutes later, my room lights up with a starry glow. Even after all the terrible things I said, Lilac Peabody's come back.

"Are you asleep?" she whispers.

I throw back my covers. "After an evening with the Reading Beauties?"

"So you finally noticed," she says sympathetically.

"It's *exactly* like *Sleeping Beauty*," I rant. "They act like they're all under a spell. They only ever snap out of it to talk about *me*. What's going on, Lilac?"

Lilac shakes her head. "Your family has got itself into a muddle, and when people get in *this* big a muddle it usually means they've lost their dreams." She gives me a mischievous smile. "And THAT'S when you call in the dream detectives! Don't you think Charlie Chase is a great name for a detective?"

I'm too upset to smile back. "I hate my name."

I say miserably. "People call you a charlie when they think you're stupid."

"I think Charlie Chase is a super-cool name," she insists. "And it's an absolutely perfect name for a stunt man!"

I stare at her. "How did you know I wanted to…"

Lilac Peabody gives me her secretive smile. "Inside info."

I feel a tiny flicker of excitement. "Are we really going to be detectives?"

"Can you think of anyone else who's smart enough to solve the Mystery of the Reading Beauties?" she chuckles.

"Actually, no," I grin. I start kidding around. "Make way for the famous dyslexic detective, Charlie Chase!"

"Oh, so it's just Charlie Chase now," she teases.

"And his trusty sidekick, of course," I tell her.

She gives me a look.

"Not a sidekick," I say hastily. "How about Charlie Chase and his otherworldly companion?"

She thinks for a minute. "That could work. Now let's go and check your parents' books," she adds unexpectedly.

I groan. "You're kidding! What are we going to learn from a bunch of mouldy books?"

Lilac gives a deep sigh. "Charlie, didn't you ever wonder what they're all reading *about*?"

We tiptoe into my parents' room.

My mum has fallen asleep with her finger inside her book. My dad's snoring with a paperback

draped over his face.

Lilac gently moves Dad's book. I switch off their reading lamps and we start snooping around.

There are wobbly stacks of books on both sides of the bed. Lilac peers at Dad's pile. "Travel books," she reports.

I squint at Mum's stack. "Love stories – yuck."

TRAVEL there and back

Lilac inspects the book dangling from Mum's hand. "This isn't a love story."

I glance at the cover. "Oh, that's just a boring gardening book."

"It is *not* just a boring gardening book!" Lilac hisses. "It's a *clue*."

"I don't think it—"

"Trust me! Your mum dreams about planting gardens."

Dad groans and rolls over. We hurry out on tiptoe.

"Maybe she *dreams* about gardens, but that's where it ends," I whisper. "Our garden's a tip. Mum only goes out to hang the washing."

"That's what makes it such a big clue," Lilac whispers back.

"So Dad likes travel books, and Mum likes love stories and gardening books," I hiss. "But what does that *prove*?"

"*Wake up*, Charlie! It tells you what's really precious to them. It tells you what they hide in their hearts."

"Keep your hair on! I didn't know, did I?"

The truth is, I'm shocked. I know kids hide stuff from their parents, but I never thought of my parents hiding stuff from me.

"Don't you wonder what your sister dreams about?" Lilac asks me.

"Probably sticking pins in me." I mutter.

But Jessie's door is locked.

I put my ear to the door. For a moment I think I hear music.

"We could get in if you used your Powers," I suggest in a low voice.

"Not allowed. Anyway, it's getting late. You've got school tomorrow."

"I won't sleep now. I'm in detecting mode," I complain.

Lilac gives me a naughty grin. "OK, let's sneak downstairs and make hot chocolate."

"All right, but I want magic marshmallows."

"Deal!"

We creep down to the kitchen.

"Detectives don't just go snooping for clues, you know," Lilac says. "They ask people questions."

I put two mugs of milk in the microwave and turn the dial.

"Lilac, get real! Who could I ask about this?"

"Your sister?"

"Yeah, and she'll go 'Mum, why is Charlie being weird? He's *talking* to me. He wants to pick a fight!'"

"Maybe she will," Lilac says softly, "and maybe she won't."

The light snaps on.

"HA! I *knew* you were up to something," says Jessie. "I heard you skulking around."

"I couldn't sleep," I say truthfully. "Thought I'd make a hot drink."

The microwave pings.

"Why did you need *two* mugs?" she asks suspiciously.

"I'm psychic – I knew you'd come downstairs."

Jessie drops into a chair. "All right, but I'll be watching your every move," she yawns. "So don't even *think* of putting salt in it."

"Jess, I was six when I did that! Six year olds think that kind of thing is funny."

I plunk a steaming mug in her hands. "Hot chocolate, no nasty surprises."

She sniffs her drink. "There'd better not be."

"Jess, did Mum and Dad always want to run a bookshop?" The question jumps out of my mouth.

My sister stares at me in amazement. "How is it you don't know something so basic?"

"But did they?"

"Of course they didn't!"

Jessie gets up and rummages on the dresser. She comes back with a photo album and flips to the first page.

"Your parents on their wedding day," she says in a bored voice.

"Yikes, check out Dad's geeky hairstyle. What *is* Mum wearing?"

She shrugs.

"Something she borrowed from one of her mates before she and Dad eloped."

My mouth falls open. "No way! They *eloped*?"

"They had to. Their parents thought they were too young to marry," Jessie explains.

"They *were* too young. They look about thirteen!"

Her eyes go dreamy. "All they owned was a mattress and an old chest of drawers. They couldn't afford to pay the electric bill, so they read poetry to each other by candlelight."

"Our parents read *poetry*?"

She grins. "And Dad played his guitar."

I howl with laughter. "Wish I'd seen that!"

"He wanted to be a songwriter." My sister pulls a face. "I found a tape." She starts to drone some lyrics. "Life is a roller coaster: gotta take the rough with the smooth, go with the flow, stay in the groove…"

I put my head in my hands. "Don't say Mum wanted to be a rock chick!"

"Actually, she wanted to be a gardener."

I'm so astonished I don't know what to say.

"Why are you staring at me?" Jessie says suspiciously. "You spat in my hot chocolate, didn't you?"

"No…" I splutter.

"You did something evil. I know you, Charlie."

Tipping her drink down the sink my sister stomps upstairs.

I throw up my hands. "And she says *I* pick fights. I mean, what's *she* got to be so angry about? My parents don't hassle *her*. They think she's Little Miss Perfect."

I'm talking to myself. Lilac Peabody has gone.

6.
THINGS TO DO BEFORE
WE GET OLD

Next day I'm the first kid out of the school gates.

I sprint home and let myself into the house. "Hiya," I call from the hall. "Just got to do some homework."

I creep into the kitchen, grab the photo album, stuff it under my sweater and dash upstairs.

I know how Mum and Dad's story starts, with poetry and candlelight, and I know how it ends, with the Reading Beauties. What I don't know is what happens in between.

I perch on my bed, flicking through pictures.
There's Mum in their back yard, tying up sweet
peas. She's got a
dirt smudge on
her nose and
a soppy grin.
And there's
Dad playing
his guitar.

Next to
him is
a book
with a
red rose
on the cover.

I might actually be a detective when I grow up, if the stuntman idea doesn't work out. I'm completely brilliant at noticing stuff – those little details that other people miss. I *know* I've seen that book before.

Tiptoeing into my parent's room, I go straight to Mum's book stack. On top is a battered book of poems with a red rose on the cover. I grab it, and scurry back to my room. My heart is hammering in my chest like bongo drums. It's almost like I know what I'm going to find.

I open the book and a sheet of note paper flutters out. It's a letter in my mum's handwriting.

"What's that?" Jessie has come in without me noticing.

"I found Mum and Dad's poetry book," I explain. "This was inside."

She peers over my shoulder. "Ooh, it's a love letter," she giggles. "Mum must have sent it to Dad before they eloped. Listen: *My darling Anthony, I know life won't be easy, but whatever happens we must hang on to our dreams…*"

Jessie breaks off, "Yuck, then it gets really lovey-dovey!" She scans the rest of the letter. "Hey, listen to this bit: *Anyway, Anthony darling, here are three things we absolutely HAVE to do before we get old and boring.*

1. Learn to dance the tango.

2. Fly over the desert in a hot-air balloon.

3. See the Indian Ocean at sunset.

"Oh my goodness! Can you picture our parents in a balloon?" Jessie sniggers.

We giggle like naughty little children.

Wow, I think. *My sister and I are actually talking!*

"Do you think they did?" I ask.

"Go up in a balloon? Nah."

"Didn't they do *any* of those things on her list?"

She shrugs. "Everyone has dreams. No one seriously expects them to come true." My sister sounds about a hundred years old.

"But *why* didn't they?" I ask.

To my dismay her face quivers. "They had kids, OK. Kids cost money. Are you happy now?"

I tell Lilac about my disturbing discovery.

"Is that how the muddle started? My parents had us and their lives turned out so boring they forgot their dreams."

She shakes her head so hard I hear her seashells tinkle.

"It's the other way round. Your parents' lives turned out boring because they forgot *how* to dream. They were so young and they tried so hard to be sensible grown-ups. They told themselves that dreams were just for children."

"Is that true?" I ask miserably. "I hate to be mean, but Dad would definitely have been a rubbish songwriter."

Lilac shakes her head again. "Then songwriting wasn't his real dream."

"But dreams *aren't* real, are they? They're all in your head."

"No, Charlie," she corrects. "Real dreams come from your heart."

I picture my mum's happy grubby face as she tied up her sweet peas, then I throw myself down on my bed.

"This mystery is too hard," I say in a muffled voice. "I feel bad about Mum and Dad but I'm only ten! What can *I* do?"

She comes to sit beside me. It's quite an experience being this close to Lilac Peabody – like being in a cool fizzy circle of sparklers.

"I'm going to tell you a secret," she whispers. "Dreams want to come true and mysteries want to be solved."

"Good luck with solving Jessie," I say gloomily. "You'll have to magic some x-ray spectacles if we want to find out what she dreams about."

Lilac grins. "Or, we could just spy on her from the garden."

"Oh, yeah. Didn't think of that!"

We creep downstairs, out of the back door and into the dark.

I follow Lilac's starry shimmer across the overgrown flowerbeds.

"Look up now," she whispers.

My sister is so worried about people coming in her door, it hasn't occurred to her that someone might look in her window. She's left the curtains wide open! Jessie's room is like a brightly lit stage as she leaps and twirls in her lonely one-girl ballet.

Don't you know anything about your family, Charlie? I think.

I'd often heard music coming from Jessie's room, but I never once suspected that it was the soundtrack to her dreams.

"Does she really want to be a dancer?" I whisper.

Lilac nods.

"So why doesn't she have lessons? If Mum and Dad knew how much…"

My sentence trails off. My parents can't afford dance lessons because they have to pay Dr Fell for my counselling sessions.

It's like trying to untangle a huge ball of string. The harder I try, the worse it gets.

Lilac has a way of reading my thoughts. "Being a dream detective is like that," she says in a sympathetic voice. "When things get this messy, it usually means you're close to solving the case.

You've got all the info. Now all you need is some really great advice!"

"OK," I say humbly. "Will you please tell me what to do, Lilac?"

She rolls her eyes. "I meant ask your mates, bird-brain!"

I'm horrified. "I'm not blabbing my business to my friends!"

She crosses her arms. "You'd help Sam, wouldn't you?"

"Of course, but—"

"And Bella has some excellent ideas – plus she likes you a *lot*," Lilac says slyly.

"But I won't know what to say."

Lilac Peabody's eyes shine like a magic cat's. "You will," she says softly. "I promise."

7.
BELLA'S PLAN

It's not easy having a private conversation in our playground. Not with footballs whizzing past your ear, or evil Honey Hope trying to eavesdrop. Luckily my mates are excellent listeners.

"Your family reads ALL the time?" Sam says in horror. "No WONDER you never invite us home."

Bella chews her plait. "Tell me those dreams again?"

I've told my friends everything. OK, not about Lilac. Come on! Would you tell *your* mates you had a little magic buddy who helps you solve your problems?

"Here's what I think," says Bella. "We can't arrange hot-air balloons or plane tickets to India. Not unless you win the lottery. But we could maybe…" Her eyes go dreamy.

"We could maybe…?" Sam hints.

Bella looks around in case Honey is still snooping. "We could *maybe* arrange a really romantic night out at a restaurant!"

"Sure!" I say. "Let's hire a stretch limo while we're at it."

"No, this could work!" Sam says eagerly. "My mum works at the Bluebird restaurant. She'll get a free table for your mum and dad no problem."

This all seems way too complicated to me.

"How would we even get them there?" I wail.

"Tell them you won a school raffle," Bella suggests, "and the prize is a three-course dinner at a fancy restaurant."

Sam frowns. "What about the tango bit? Dancing the tango is the whole point!"

"Hold your horses, Sam Sparks," Bella says. "My aunt and uncle are super-brilliant dancers, OK? And they owe me big time for baby-sitting Emerald."

I stare at her. "Seriously? Your aunt and uncle would really give my parents a free tango lesson?"

"Why not? They gave me a free circus in the park!" grins Sam.

Bella's eyes sparkle. "The *instant* Charlie's mum and dad finish their coffee, Sam's mum goes over and tells them there's another, mystery, prize. Then the music starts and my uncle and aunt come out and sweep them off their feet!"

I feel a smile spread across my face.

"There's just one thing," Bella says. "The Bluebird is incredibly posh. Have your parents got any posh clothes?"

I picture my parents in their tired old sweatshirts and jeans. "Not really."

"Then you've *got* to get your sister in on it," Bella says firmly. "Tell her your dad has to wear a suit and your mum has to wear a *really* sexy dress!"

Sam gets out his notebook. "So shall I get Mum to reserve a table for Friday night?"

For the second time in history I run all the way home.

I peek round the sitting room door. The Reading Beauties are in their usual positions. Martha looks up from her little board book.

"Huwwo," she says softly.

This HAS to work. I absolutely refuse to let my cute little sister be turned into a Reading Beauty, even if this means asking my angry big sister for help.

"Jess," I hiss. "I need to talk to you."

She doesn't even bother to reply, just holds her book up in front of her face. I can see the picture on the cover: two smiling girls in tutus.

The clues were in front of me all the time, yet I never even noticed until Lilac Peabody pointed them out.

"Jess, it's important!"

Something in my voice makes her look up.

She puts her book down, yawning. "This had better not be one of your stunts!"

"It isn't, I swear."

I practically drag her upstairs.

When we're safely in my room, I take out Mum's letter, then I get a pen and circle the first item on her dream list.

Jessie gasps. "What are you *doing?*"

"I'm saving this family's dreams," I tell her. "And you're helping."

I'm ready to bully her, blackmail her, *anything* to get our parents down to the Bluebird restaurant next Friday.

But when my sister hears our plan she's ecstatic! "Mum and Dad are going to LOVE it!" she yells. " I can't believe you thought of this, Charlie."

"Sssh! They'll hear you," I hiss. "What about the

sexy dress? Does Mum actually *own* a dress?"

"No problem," Jessie says. "Sarah's mum wears super-cool clothes. I'm sure she's got something Mum can borrow."

Maybe Lilac's Powers are catching, because Bella's plan suddenly has a life of its own. All these people are chipping in to help. People I don't even know, like Sarah's mum and Bella's auntie and uncle!

"Can you do something with Mum's hair?" I ask anxiously. "And Dad mustn't wear that hideous sweater. He has to wear a suit."

"I told you. I'll *sort* it," she says. "So when are you telling them?"

This is the tricky bit. Suppose my bookworm parents are in such a rut they'd actually turn down a free meal at a five-star restaurant?

"We should tell them now," my sister says. "It'll give me more time for the big makeover."

"They'll say they can't get a baby-sitter," I hiss on the stairs. "Tell them you'll do it. Tell them you'll ring them on their mobile if there's an emergency."

"Tell them yourself," Jessie hisses back. "It's your plan."

She practically boots me into the sitting room.

My parents look up in surprise.

"Mum, Dad," I say breathlessly, "I want to tell you something."

Mum's forehead crinkles. "Is something—"

"Nothing's wrong," I say hastily. I clear my throat. "How would you like a night out at the Bluebird?"

"Very funny," says Dad.

"I'm serious. I won top prize in the school raffle."

"You won dinner at the Bluebird?" they gasp.

"Yeah, but it's not really my thing. I thought you guys might like to go. Sam's mum's got you a table for this Friday."

My parents look stunned, and a tiny bit scared.

"But what about—" Mum starts.

"I'll baby-sit," Jessie says at once. "You two haven't been out for ages."

"What do you think?" Dad mutters to Mum.

"Anthony, I can't! I haven't got anything to—"

"I can get you the perfect dress," Jessie says eagerly. "And I know exactly how to do your hair. Say you'll go. Please?"

"But why—" Mum starts.

"I don't actually care why, Claire," Dad interrupts. He looks unusually determined. "Tell Sam's mum we'll be there," he tells me.

Jessie and I exchange delighted glances.

"Cool!" I tell them.

But when Thursday night comes our plan doesn't seem nearly so cool.

"They won't know what to talk about!" I wail. "They'll end up getting a divorce and it'll be all my fault!"

Lilac pats my pillow. "You and Jessie are doing great," she says. "And don't forget, I'll be there tomorrow too."

"Really? You're actually going to the restaurant?" I perk up.

"Charlie, I wouldn't miss it for the world," she says softly.

8.
THE KEY TO EVERYTHING

On Friday night my parents set off to the Bluebird, looking like scared strangers in their borrowed clothes.

We give Martha a bath and dress her in her

little sleep suit. Then we play endless games to keep her amused, but we can't quite seem to relax.

"How long have they been gone now?" I ask.

"Nearly an hour," Jessie sighs.

Thirty more minutes drag by.

"I can't take this," Jessie says suddenly. "I've got to see if they're all right."

I giggle with relief. "Me too."

"We'll whizz down to check on them and whizz straight back," she says.

"Martha won't tell, will you Marth?" I grin.

We bundle our baby sister into her fluffy coat, strap her in the buggy and wheel her out into the cold starry night.

"Dark!" Martha says happily. "Moon! Stars!"

"Save some words for tomorrow, shorty!" I tell her.

When we reach the Bluebird we almost lose

our nerve. Luckily Sam's mum spots us crossing the road. She opens a side door and beckons us in. "Is everything OK?"

"We were just passing," I fib, "and we wondered if our parents had started their tango lesson yet?"

"Can't you hear the music?" She touches her heart. "Oh, it's *so* romantic."

A man's voice floats from an open door. "Anthony, you must be strong and proud like a lion!"

"And you are the lioness, Claire!" says a woman's voice.

"Ouch," says my mum. "The lion just trampled on my toes!"

"Sorry, this is harder than it looks."

We peep around the door in time to see Dad fall over his own feet. "Ow! Sorry," he says again.

It's all going horribly wrong.

"Mumma," says a little voice.

Somehow my baby sister has escaped from her buggy. She can't walk yet, but she can crawl faster than you'd ever believe! She zooms between my legs and into the room, yelling, "Mumma, Mumma!"

Jessie and I rush in after her.

"Sorry, sorry, this SO wasn't meant to happen!" Jessie wails.

"Where did you spring from?" my dad demands.

"Have you come to learn the tango?" Bella's auntie beams at us.

"We wanted to make sure everyone was having a good time," I explain lamely.

To my astonishment Mum throws her arms around me. "Charlie, we're having a *wonderful* time. Of course it would be better if we could get your father to stop treading on his own feet!" she giggles. "But Louisa and Pedro are such good teachers."

"We always wanted to learn," Dad says to Bella's uncle. "But somehow…"

They look like different people. Happy, breathless, and surprisingly groovy in their borrowed clothes.

They woke up! I think wonderingly. My mum and dad remembered their dreams and they woke up from the evil Reading Beauties spell!

"So, we'll see you back home then?" I say shyly.

"Well, eventually," says Dad.

"Yes, don't wait up!" smiles Mum.

Jessie giggles in my ear. "Little brother, our work is done."

"Yeah," I whisper. "Now it's up to them."

In real life you don't get big happy endings, just new beginnings.

One day I come home to find my parents lugging boxes of books out to the car.

"What's going on?" I say.

"We're making space," Mum says briskly. "You can't *move* in there without falling over old books."

"Your mum and I decided we're just going to concentrate on travel books from now on," Dad explains.

"Correction," Mum smiles, "*you're* concentrating on travel books. I'm going back to college!"

I gulp. "You are?"

"I'm going to study landscape gardening," Mum announces proudly. "I'm still going to help your dad write his book though."

My mouth drops open. "Dad's writing a book?"

"I've always wanted to write my own travel book," he says. "Your mum and I thought we'd write one together. Of course, we'll have to do some research."

"Fancy spending next Christmas in India?" Mum grins.

They go inside for another load, almost colliding with Jessie.

"Move, Charlie!" she yells, barging past. "Miss Goodwin is going to *kill* me!"

I watch my sister race down the street, clutching her new dance bag. She looks furious, but I know she's just stressing about being late, not truly mad like before.

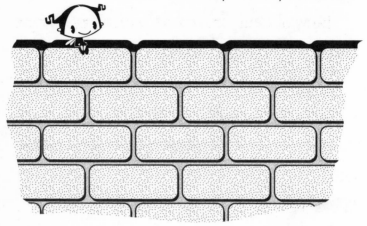

"I think our case is closed, don't you?" says a voice.

A shimmery little figure is sitting on the garden wall.

I know she's come to say goodbye, but I try to play it cool.

"Yeah! Peabody and Chase did a good job."

"They *are* an excellent team," she agrees smugly.

I don't know what to say. Lilac Peabody helped me get my family back. Just saying "thank you" doesn't seem like enough.

"Detectives don't hug, do they?" I ask her huskily.

She puts her head on one side like a shimmery bird. "Detectives can hug if they like."

Hugging Lilac Peabody feels like diving into a bath of extra-fizzy ginger beer! We do our nutty handshake one last time, then Lilac gives me her look, as if she's seeing the past, present and future Charlie Chase all at once. "Maybe you should give books a second chance," she suggests softly. "Now everyone else is going with the flow."

"You've been listening to Dad's lyrics!" I grin.

Lilac starts singing Dad's terrible rock song and I join in.

"Life is a roller coaster:
Gotta take the rough with the smooth,
Gotta go with the flow,
Stay in the groove."

When we get to the last line Lilac blows me a kiss. Then she's gone, leaving a faint shimmer that only I can see.

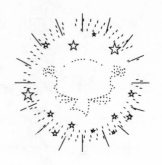

Dad struggles out with a box. "What's that you were singing?" he puffs.

"Oh, just some old song," I tell him. "Dad, that's too heavy. Let me help!"

I'm only helping my parents carry boxes, but it feels magic. For the first time, everyone in my family is living in the same world. If you ask me, that's the *real* Key to Everything: everyone in the same world, dreaming the same dream.